Across The Universe
Not Really a Beatles Story

By
Robbie Sheerin

Robbiesheerinwriter.com

PRINT ISBN 978-1737931065

Cover design by: Robbie Sheerin and Silly Lilly Publishing
Printed in the United States of America

Other books by this author

The Orb
Bite Sized Fiction
Tales From Another Dimension
The Last Job
Fractured Memory

Contents

1
Yer Blues

I sit in the waiting room of the doctor's office as the subtle smell of disinfectant tries to squeeze through my stuffy nose. I'm surrounded by germ-infested and disease-ridden souls, but I'm strategically positioned safely away from those who looked the worst—the ones with the hacking, flemmy coughs and hot, sweaty foreheads.

The wait is long, and I should have been looked at first, because let's face it, I'm better than these folks, and I'm a busy man. My throat aches, and my headache is making me dizzy. Every time I cough, it hurts.

I go back to finishing the half-completed crossword in a newspaper. I've always been good at games, especially word searches, crosswords, and Scrabble. I once won an anagram contest in Reader's Digest two years in a row.

"Mr. Moody?" calls a pudgy nurse from across the room. He has red cheeks and obnoxiously spiked red hair like a hedgehog. Hey buddy, the Sex Pistols are asking for their haircut back.

I cough gingerly, trying to clear my throat without causing any more pain. It's murder. "Yes, I'm here."

"Dr. Macintosh will see you now," the hedgehog mutters.

Finally!

After explaining my symptoms fully to the doctor, he takes the customary swab of the inside of my red, inflamed mouth and leaves the room.

I wait. Again.

He returns a few minutes later. "Well, Mr. Moody, your strep test came back negative. It seems you have the old curse of the common cold," says the grey-haired doctor as he slouches down into his worn-out brown leather chair.

"Are you sure, doc? Because I feel like total crap."

It must be more than the common cold. Mixing with all those people at the office party yesterday, hugging and dancing, people sharing those red solo cups, most likely with some sickly sod who should have stayed home that day. I could have picked up anything!

He clasps his hands together, making a triangle, and smiles. "Yes, I am sure. I did not go to school for seven years to not know the difference between strep and the common cold, Mr. Moody."

He looks at me over the top of his gold-rimmed glasses, studying me like my grandfather used to do when he was trying to catch me in a lie. It is a stare of intimidation. It works, I guess I will concede.

"Fine, what are you going to prescribe me?"

"The best medicine for the common cold is plenty of fluids and rest, Mr. Moody."

"That's it!?"

Oh boy, this guy needs to go back to medical school. That's not treatment. I no longer concede; this could be life or death!

"What about a steroid or an antibiotic?!" I pleaded.

"Mr. Moody," he says firmly, with a sense of impatience. "Antibiotics fight bacteria; they do not fight viruses. And steroids are not—for the common cold."

"Fine, I guess I will just let my body slowly fight its way out of this hell. I hope I can pull through, Doc."

"I am confident you will, Mr. Moody." His impatient voice now had the subtle tone of sarcasm. Was he mocking me?

"How's the job at the newspaper going, and weren't you writing a book the last time I saw you?

"Yes, I'm still at the newspaper and still doing research for my Beatles book. Let me tell you something, Doc, there would be a lot less love in this world if it were not for the Beatles and their timeless music."

"I suppose you might be correct there, Mr. Moody. And are you still moonlighting as a PI?"

"Yup. In fact, I'm investigating…." I cup my mouth and lower my voice. "Quarrymen Insurance."

"Did they not have some insider trading concerns, bankruptcy, and changes in their management?"

"Oh yes. A mess, in fact, an enigmatic entanglement!"

"It seems you're a busy man, Mr. Moody. But I want you to take it easy for the next couple of days." He points a crooked finger at me. "Go home and rest. You never know when the next big adventure will be, and you will need your strength."

I leave the doctor's office not feeling any better than when I went in. So much for modern medicine.

I pass a hacking mother with bright red hair and her freckled daughter in the doorway. They are both tall and skinny, with dark eyes and high cheekbones. They could have passed as sisters;

maybe they were. Who cares, I avoid them. Not for their safety, but for mine. I use my sleeve to hold the door handle as they pass me.

When I swallow, it's like I have a hundred needles lodged in my throat, going in every which way. My head throbs like it's ready to explode like a puss filled pimple. I hope I don't have a brain tumor. Could I have a brain tumor? I should make an appointment.

Slowly, I drag myself along the stone pathway to the parking lot like a leper. I feel like I should be ringing a bell and calling out, 'unclean, unclean.' My head feels so hot, and my body aches like I have just endured twelve rounds with Mike Tyson. Not the Jake Paul-Mike Tyson, but a Tony Tucker-Mike Tyson.

A light mist of rain begins to fall on my face. It feels good, cooling my fiery, hot forehead. As I get to my car, the mist turns into droplets, and then once in my car, it begins to downpour as the heavens open, like the days of Noah. Within a few minutes, dirty puddles are forming.

There is nothing worse than having a blinding headache and having to drive in the rain while hampered by foggy car windows. I start the engine and sit there as the heater defogs my windshield. My phone beeps, and I look to see a text message from Monica, a work colleague. She's a little annoying. I mean, she's texted me twice already, asking how I feel and if I need anything. That's annoying, right?

Yer Blues plays on the radio. I turn the volume down low, but still hear the lyrics over the tapping of the rain on the roof. Yeah, John, I do feel like dying. Finally, the window is clear. But just as I'm about to drive off, a woman in a long black coat and black boots appears out of nowhere. I slam on the brakes.

"Idiot! Watch where you're going!"

The blond-haired woman stands there as droplets of rain run off her coat. She glares at me through her wet blonde hair, which partially covers her face. Her scowl is cold and unflinching. She glances to the left and right before walking off. How peculiar—something feels wrong, unnerving, something out of place, like seeing a fox during the day or a discarded couch at the edge of a highway.

I make my way home, hoping no one else ignorantly steps in front of my car. It would be their fault, though; I am clearly sick and suffering from some sort of obscure illness. Plus, roads are for cars, not people!

There's a break in the clouds, and the rain relents as I pull up to my house. Exiting the car, I glance up at the dark clouds above. A dreaded sign of an impending storm rolling in from the sea.

Hello, Edmond," comes the annoying, piercing voice of my neighbor over the yapping of her irritating Yorkshire terrier. I hate that dog.

I turn to see her at the edge of my driveway. Her little devil dog has mounted the wall, barking, ready to invade the land beyond its own kingdom. One day, I will drop-kick that mutt deep into the woods. And her dog.

"Hello Mrs. Thomson," I say lazily. I hide my rolling eyes, a knee-jerk reaction. I give a floppy, halfhearted wave. My arm has no strength to it, clearly this ravaging disease is wasting away at my muscles.

I avoid chatting with her—the neighborhood gossip. No doubt she wants to tell me all about Fred's overly populated strawberry bushes and Mrs. Clayton's new windows, which she can't possibly afford as a widow. I would never get those minutes back from her pointless blathering. Spend my last moments listening to her? No, thank you. I vanish into the sanctuary of my house.

I'm welcomed by the meows of a cat.

"Yes, yes, I see you."

Mr. Ringo sits on the stairs, crying for his water bowl to be replenished. The large ginger cat, like most felines, believes he is the master and lord of the manor, and all others are there to serve him. I am the biggest sucker for him; he is better than most humans I know. After filling his water and food bowls, I ascend the stairs to my bedroom, put on my Beatles pajamas, and climb into bed, or maybe my deathbed, who knows.

Mr. Ringo wanders inquisitively into the bedroom, surveying his kingdom and deciding where he wants to sleep next.

I grimace and close my eyes as I swallow my collection of rusty needles.

"Goodbye, Mr. Ringo, you've been a good friend."

He looks at me with those judgmental eyes and that stuck-up nose before turning and leaving the room, deciding he doesn't want to share it with such a sickly human as me. I can't blame him, neither would I.

I reach into my nightstand and remove a bottle of red cough syrup. Ah, yummy syrup. I down a couple of caps full of thick and sweet liquid. I snuggle into my pillows, allowing the syrup to do its job. It gets to work fast, blocking histamines. My eyelids begin to feel heavy. Sleep comes rapidly.

2

I'm Only Sleeping

I slowly open my eyes. I should say, 'eye,' only one really opens. The green LED clock on the nightstand glows like a piece of kryptonite in a dark cave. The time reads 3;35am.

Light flashes from behind my curtains. Moments later, the cracks of thunder echo outside. I can hear Mr. Ringo scampering around in the hallway, no doubt seeking the safety of some cat-bomb-shelter. The wind and rain howl outside, making me shiver, causing me to retreat into the warmth of my covers as I close my eyes. I pull the heavy blanket back over my head. Bye bye, nasty weather.

***

I sit in a low, worn-out tweed chair in Twickenham Studios, next to Michael Lindsay-Hogg and Linda McCartney. The smell of a cigar wafts by me from a nearby smoker. It's 1969, and the Fab Four sit huddled in a large room. Various colored lights illuminate the walls behind them, giving a trippy ambient vibe. Paul and John discuss the lyrics to a new song, while Yoko sits wearing a fur coat, reading the London Times. Ringo sips a cup of tea and sits patiently, waiting to play a drum beat. I feel like I am part of history, staring at legends creating memories for millions of fans. I find it funny that the words they sing, "love lasts forever," and knowing these very songs will last forever.

***

I wake up to the morning light as the sun shines through the gaps between the curtains and the window frame, casting sunbeams across my room. I swallow, seems like there are fewer needles in my throat today. My headache has almost gone, and the fist punching inside my skull trying to escape has turned into a dull tap. Anything is better than yesterday.

I guess the doctor might have been right. But I still reserve a level of doubt as to his qualifications as a medical practitioner. But for now, I am on the mend. Swinging my legs out of bed and sitting upright, I stretch toward the ceiling, bringing life back into my joints and muscles. It feels good.

I open my curtains and peer out into the void, wondering what damage the storm has wrenched on the world outside. A couple of large branches lay across a neighbor's lawn, like fallen soldiers of the Treefolk. Some rogue trash barrels gently rock on their sides in the middle of the street. Thankfully, all the large trees and power lines are where they should be.

My eyes are drawn to movement in Mrs. Thomson's backyard. She stands with her back to me.

Her dog suddenly appears.

I rub my eyes. This can't be real! I must be delirious from the cough syrup,

Her dog is not a dog at all. It's a large, furry black and gray beast with bulging muscles. It's bigger than a Yorkshire Terrier and still has a leash around it, pressing tightly into its fat, furry neck. It turns and looks at me, its large fangs dripping with saliva. Burning red eyes stare at me, and for a moment, we lock eyes in some disturbing staring contest of horror. I duck down and fall to the floor.

Maybe it didn't see me! No, you idiot, it saw you! Is this a nightmare?

I slowly approach the window again and hesitantly peer outside. I involuntarily let out a gasp as my sweaty fingers slip off the windowsill. A new sight, a new nightmare. What should have been Mrs. Thomson is now some grotesque and inhuman abomination. Her eyes are sunken into her face. Her teeth and jawbones showing through her tightly pulled skin.

I feel my headache building, a dull pain behind my eyeball. None of this makes any sense. I try to process what I've just seen. I can't bear to look out the window again, but I have to. Then I notice a rapid scratching sound from the hallway. I try to slow my breathing and listen. It must be Mr. Ringo. My legs feel weak, I don't think I can stand, never mind walk. So I crawl to the bedroom door on all fours, like a scared, defenseless animal.

"Mr. Ringo?" I say, my voice unsure and shaky.

As I peer around the door into the hallway, what I see makes me recoil. Mr. Ringo is not Mr. Ringo—he is no longer a cat at all. Instead, he is a small, fat child on his hands and knees. What the heck. He is covered in ginger fur. Much of his face is orange skin, sounded in what looks like a lion's mane. His hands, or paws, end in huge six-inch talons that click against the wooden floor as he moves.

He snarls at me. His whiskers move as he sniffs the air, smelling his prey—me. He runs at me, click, click, click, as he picks up speed. I immediately kick the door closed. A second later, there is a powerful thud from behind the door.

"I'm gonna die, I'm gonna die!"

Adrenaline is now soaring through my system, powering my legs as I spring to my feet and run to the bathroom. Fumbling for the bolt, I lock the door behind me and jump into the bathtub, hoping it will somehow protect me like a force field, cocooning me from danger. What the heck is going on here? Mrs. Thomson, her scary devil dog, and now poor Mr. Ringo. This world is not mine. Not earth. And how do I get back!? Am I dreaming? I have to be dreaming! I slap my face hard.

"Wake up!" Get it together, Edmond, get it together."

I step from the bathtub and peer into the mirror. Sweat covers my forehead as droplets slowly ran down the length of my hair onto my pajama shirt. My face burns red-hot, like a marathon runner's face on a summer's day.

There's suddenly a loud crack of wood crunching and splintering. It must be my bedroom door. It didn't hold for long. Then I heard the click, click, click of the trotting beast on the floor, searching my room, no doubt looking for me.

Panic is setting in; my heart races and pounds within my chest. The whirling sound of blood racing in my eardrums feels nauseating. I scan the room for weaponry, but it's a bathroom, not an armory on a military base!

Finally, surrendering to some pathetic armaments—a plunger and a laundry basket cover made of wicker. I brace myself for an attack and hold the bathroom door handle. I look at the weapons in my hand, it's a far cry from Sir Lancelot. My confidence wanes. Maybe I can fit through the window and escape? Nope, it's too small. It's not like in the movies; I would never make it out that tiny hole in the wall they call a window. I glance around the bathroom, looking for other options.

Then it comes to me.

I listen for the click, click, click, trying to surmise where the beast is. Once I feel it's close enough, I swing the door open. The beast turns its head, and before it can attack, I throw my plastic shower curtain over it. It thrashes, its vision obscured. I grab the shower curtain rod from the doorway and bring it down hard on its head.

There's a sickly, muffled crack beneath the plastic curtain, and the outline of the creature collapses. I'm not sure if I've killed it or knocked it out. For a moment, it feels strange that I may have just killed a living creature, and that I happened to have a shower curtain handy. Tony Soprano, are you impressed, sir? The thought disappears as quickly as the beast stirs beneath the plastic sheet.

I exit the room in a panic and make my way downstairs, almost falling in my frenzied attempt to leap down multiple stairs. That's all I need, a broken ankle, a virus, and maybe a brain tumor, while being chased by a beast that once was my cat.

I need to get out of the house. It's no longer safe, no longer a haven of comfort or isolation. It's a torture chamber where a nightmare has been unleashed upon its victim.

My car! I need to get to the safety of my car. How fast could Mr. Ringo, or whatever that thing is, run? I'm sure it's not fast enough. Then again, anything was possible, Mrs. Thomson, her devil dog, and now my ginger boy-cat.

I slip on my shoes, grab my car keys, and flee the house. Cold air hits my face, earthy and musty. There's an eerie silence, no birds, no wind, no cars in the neighborhood. It's as if the world is void of life except for the beast in my house, and next door.

I run to the car while glancing around for any threats. My run turns into a walk when I see what looks like giant strawberry vines stretching up higher than the streetlights. Long stems with giant, furry berries. It looks like something from Jack and the Beanstalk, except for the strawberries on top. Below, large strawberries lay in a field. Strawberry fields forever?

I realize I am standing in my driveway, gawking, staring at Fred's strawberry bushes. Nothing makes any sense. I quickly reach my car and get inside. The pain behind my eyeball is now becoming a full-blown migraine. I feel nauseous, and I momentarily think about the possibility of a brain tumor again. It must be a brain tumor! This is all a symptom of a brain tumor!

Suddenly, a hand tries to get into the locked passenger side door. I look to see who it is. The blonde hair of a woman hangs down from her tilted head. Her beautiful emerald-green eyes locked onto mine. To my surprise, it's the blonde I had almost ran over outside the doctor's office. I freeze, not sure what to do.

"If you want to live, let me in now," she says firmly, in an American accent.

I find myself reaching for the button to unlock the doors, but I hesitate, unsure of trusting this total stranger, regardless of how attractive she is. She just stands there staring at me, willing me to open the door.

Either this blonde was going to kill me, the devil dog, or Mr. Ringo. I decide she is the least scary option, and I'd rather a beautiful woman kill me than be mauled by a couple of wild beasts. I press the button, releasing all the door locks. Gathering the tails of her long coat, the stranger climbs into the front seat and slams the door shut.

She stares straight ahead and points. "Drive."

Just then, Mrs. Thomson's devil dog leaps onto the hood of the car, its claws scratching the blue paintwork of my Honda Civic as it stalks toward the windshield.

"We're gonna die! We're gonna die! We are going to die!!"

I let out an uncontrolled yelp, of which I am instantly embarrassed. The blonde once again says, "Drive."

I slam the car into drive and floor it, causing the devil dog to lose grip and tumble off the hood. We leave my driveway, tires squealing and spinning, smashing into the trash barrels in the street.

"Where are we going?"

"The reservoir."

3

Magical Mystery Tour

"The reservoir? Why there? No, no, no, we need to go to the police, the feds, and the army! We need to go.."

"They are all compromised," Blondie rudely interrupts.

"Compromised? What do you mean, compromised?"

"Look, Edmond!"

She said that, like my mother. And how did she know my name?

"Everything you think you know about your world, your planet, the people, it's all an illusion. You live one life, see one world, and travel one timeline. But you're a tiny speck in the universe, in dozens of universes, in fact."

I brake hard, causing the woman to thrust her hands against the dashboard. I slide the car into park and turn to the stranger.

"I am not going anywhere until you tell me who you are. What's going on? And how do you know my name?"

I turn away, defiantly folding my arms, and sit staring out of the window. I'm not moving until I get answers. She looks out of her door window and then out of the rear window, then turns and faces me. I ignore her and keep looking straight ahead.

"Look, I understand this is a lot for you to process. But right now, this is not the time or place to sit here and talk about it. If you can, please take me to the reservoir. I will explain there. If, after I have explained everything to you, you choose to leave, you can, and just view this as giving me a ride."

She has a point. I guess. What is the rush? Maybe it was my impatience that was the problem, but unlikely, because I am right most of the time. Clearly, something was wrong in the world, and it was not going to just correct itself overnight. What was one hour longer?

I put the car into drive and head toward the highway. The woman is nonchalantly calm for what seems like the earth momentarily slipping off its axis. Such oddities would jar overgrown strawberry bush monstrosities, scary wild creatures, and my mummified neighbor. Although I would never voice this, I am slightly envious of her relaxed disposition. Something Monica has politely and annoyingly stated that I would be wise to cultivate. But then again, what does she know?

We turn onto Main Street, and it's oddly quiet, the stillness eerie and uncomfortable. I feel the hairs on the back of my damp back stand up. Fear tingling in my fingertips, and they grip the steering wheel. There's no cars or even people. It's like driving on Christmas Day; while the world stuffs its faces with turkey and wine, the roads, highways, and parks lay barren and desolate.

I become aware—for how long, I'm not sure—that my mouth is hanging open as I gawk at the entire buildings missing on Main Street.

"Shears."

"What?" replied Blondie.

"Shears."

"Oh, your barber shop," she says matter-of-factly.

"Yes, it's vanished."

The building has completely disappeared from among adjoining buildings, like a slice of wedding cake carefully exhumed with a knife. Gaps lay where apartments and stores once sat, leaving exposed foundations behind.

Then I had a puzzling thought.

"How did you know Shears was my barber shop? Have you been stalking me?"

"I have been tracking you."

"Tracking me, stalking me, it's the same thing, girly."

"Don't call me girly."

"Then what do I call you?"

"My name is Adlin."

Our conversation ends when another incomprehensible site steals my attention.

The old cobblestone clock tower in the city square has been replaced with a Swiss chalet, styled with a large, disproportional gabled roof, extra-wide matching eves, and exposed wooden beams. I half expect the Von Trapp family to exit the front door and begin singing that the hills are alive with the sound of music.

All the streetlights and road signs have sunk, leaving the lights and stop signs less than two feet from the ground. Adlin pulls a device from inside her jacket pocket. It's larger than an iPhone but smaller than an iPad. She taps and swipes the screen.

"Seventy-one hours," she mumbles to herself.

I don't bother asking what she's doing. I just want to ditch her and find the police. We finally reach the highway, and I take the ramp southbound toward Graven Woods. The highway is just as bizarre as downtown Graven. The grass along the roadside is folded over and flattened, like wet, combed hair.

I notice brown patches randomly scattered across the grass. As I focus on them, something remarkable occurs to me: they are clumps of porphyria! Which makes zero sense. How can there be cold water seaweed here? We are miles from the ocean.

We pass a sign on the highway that reads: "Graven Reservoir – 2 Miles."

I wrote an article about the reservoir for the newspaper a few years ago about ground erosion and animal habitats. That was the most exciting news Graven ever seemed to produce. This new mystery is different. Something that will test my investigative experience and instincts. Piecing it together will be more challenging than tracking down a runaway kid. But I was the best reporter on the paper—probably the best. And it would take that kind of work to solve this. The police will be glad to know their best investigator is on the job.

Glancing in the mirror, I immediately sit up. Is that a car in the distance? I strain for a few moments, but yes, it's a car! Maybe other normal people running from the madness. Or maybe not; perhaps they are like Mrs. Thomson.

The car approaches, and as the vehicle pulls alongside, I am overwhelmed with horror. The driver and passenger look just like Mrs. Thompson, with jaundice-colored skin pulled tightly over their faces. They stared at me with bloodshot eyes, set into grotesque, bulging, and inflamed sockets.

As I look at the ghoulish characters next to me, my car veers slightly off the road.

"Stay focused, Edmond, eyes on the road. They can't see us," Adlin says flatly.

I jerk the car back onto the road and refocus.

"Okay, gir-". "I mean, Adlin, they can't see us?"

"Yes, I have created a temporal time field around us, masking our appearance."

"Say what? Never mind, you'll tell me at the reservoir."

Can't wait to ditch her. She might be beautiful, but she's a little loco.

4

Lucy in the Sky with Diamonds

We exit the highway, and it only takes a few minutes before we reach the parking lot of the reservoir. It's empty, of course, just like the lifeless town of Graven. It's a beautiful view of the dam and reservoir from the slightly elevated parking lot. It makes me smile. It's a reminder of the norm, and normality was something that had been absent today.

The dam splits the landscape into two different worlds: a valley of lush green fields and trees below, and a vast sheet of water above. Covered in black algae and moss, the stone structure stretches four hundred feet across the expanse, dividing land from reservoir.

Centered in the middle of the dam is a small control tower. The windows provide a three-hundred-and-sixty-degree view of the surroundings as they wrap around the round tower, two floors high. With the effects of time and oxide erosion, the once shiny copper domed roof is now a blue-green patina color, and no longer reflects the bright sun.

The dam is wide enough for a car to pass over, between two four-foot walls that line the edges of the dam. Large black wrought-iron gates block both ends, restricting any vehicles from crossing the dam.

I conjure a stern voice. "Now you can tell me why you've been stalking me and how you know my name."

"Okay, Edmond."

She looks down at her device before peering upward out of the front window, then the passenger side window.

"Edmond, do you believe in multiple dimensions?"

"As in, time and space?"

"Yes!" she says excitedly.

"No, I do not. Don't be ridiculous. You can't go back in time to things that have already happened, and you can't go to the future where things haven't happened."

"I am not talking about time travel. Your mind wouldn't be able to fathom that concept. No, I mean other worlds that run parallel to yours."

"That's just as ridiculous as time travel."

"As ridiculous as your cat turning into a raging beast? As unbelievable as Graven missing entire buildings?"

Hmm, she has a point there, and once again, I find myself conceding to her. She's a stranger, but I'm drawn to her in some odd way, like our paths have crossed or we have something in common.

"Okay, you have two minutes to explain everything."

She turns in her chair, tucking her hair behind both ears. I can see the intensity in her green eyes.

"Imagine, for a moment, that the universe is broken up into aisles, all lined up next to each other."

"Like a grocery store?"

"Yes. Each aisle has its own timeline. One, where there are pets that look like wild ravenous creatures and mummified people, large strawberry bushes, tiny trees, and worlds almost entirely made of oceans."

"One with my barber shop and the weird Von Trapp family house?"

"Yes. Now imagine that the shelving and partitions that separate the aisles crack or expand, creating gaps that allow objects and living things to bleed into other realities. This, is what has happened here."

I process that for a moment. Okay, a little longer than a moment. "I guess it's possible, maybe, in a weird Stephen Hawkings kind of way. But how do you know all this?"

"I'm from one of these other realities. I have been tracking you because you have been identified as unique."

Yes, I know that I'm unique. "Unique, in what way?"

"Your actions and life have been marked as a permanence of time."

"A what of time?"

She glances out of the window again, as if looking for something.

"A permanence of time is a set time when a multitude of actions and occurrences take place because of your actions. Your choices affect people all over the world in this dimension and others. It can't be quantified or even explained. But simply put, you must survive this reality, or events will cease to exist in dozens of other realities, changing history."

Ha! I've found a flaw in her logic. "If there are barriers or partitions that separate our worlds, how can my choices affect the residents of other worlds?"

"If someone like you nudges these partitions, you cause an effect. Like bumping into a stranger behind a curtain."

I can't help but laugh. "So, no pressure at all then?"

She slams her hand down on the dashboard, making me jump.

"This is serious!"

Her face flushes with anger. She means business. She means every word of this crazy talk.

Blinking rapidly, I try to process everything. It makes sense; I understood the concept, but could it really happen? Are there whole other worlds outside our own? My headache begins knocking within my skull again. The idea creates a lump in my lingering, itchy throat.

"So, what you're saying is-," I can't believe I'm about to actually say this, "that these creatures and anomalies have bled into my world?"

"No, Edmond. You have fallen into theirs."

5

With a Little Help from My Friends

My mouth goes completely dry, like I have taken a spoonful of flour, soaking up every molecule of moisture inside my mouth cavity. I can feel my heart race, adrenaline soars within my body, causing me to overheat; sweat beads on my forehead. Here comes that old fight-or-flight state, I guess. My nauseating headache returns. My grip on reality is slipping, as if greased with oil.

I suddenly feel a hand touch me, and I instantly relaxed. I look down to see Adlin's hand resting on mine.

"I am going to help you get back to your world, Edmond," she says in a soothing voice.

Unbelievable as this situation was, I find myself believing and trusting her. She has plausible answers, even if they were wildly imaginative. "So, what do we do?"

She again is distracted by the device in her hand, as if waiting for something to appear on the screen.

She turns to me and says, "Just like in your universe, there are units of the government and military, often coalescing with each other, that investigate, and study things that are outside the realm of the norm: UFOs, intelligent life, other dimensions, and space travel. These aspects are often hidden from the fearful public but known to the Area 51 nuts and conspiracists."

I nod in agreement. As a journalist, I've heard and read the wild claims and stories of alien abductions, found mostly in the pages of the Weekly World News and The Roswell Observer. Even the best reporters, like me, of course, keep tabs on popular tabloids, even if they were outlandish and ludicrous.

The day is now noticeably darker; the sky becoming overcast. Black clouds appear over the hills, seemingly moving toward us. Leafs skim and dance across the parking lot in circular motions.

"Although we were hidden from passersby on the highway, your neighbor would have contacted the authorities. And coupled with the storm, these special government entities will have been on high alert for any anomalies."

"You mean the storm was not a storm?"

"Well, it was, but it was more than just a weather event. Even your flu-like symptoms were not because of a virus or sickness. That was your body dealing with the impending absorbance into this dimension.”

And the wildly unimaginable revelations just keep coming. Even Paul and the rest of the Fab Four couldn't dream of a psychedelic trip as this was turning out to be.

“Okay.”

Her device chirps as if getting an alert. Her eyes dart to the screen. “We need to go, now!”

As I reach to turn the ignition, she opens the car door. A gust of wind rushes inside.

“On foot, let's go!”

I exit the car and jog to catch up with her. We walk toward the dam. The wind picks ups, and lightning strikes the earth in the distance.

I felt like a fool out in the open, dressed in pajamas and my sneakers. It's a fleeting thought, though; there are worse things in the world, you know, like falling into another dimension!

“Where are we going, Adlin? What's going on?”

“Those black clouds, the wind,” she points skyward, “that's not a storm. That's another barrier about to open.”

“From my world?” Maybe I can go home.

“Unfortunately, no.”

Adlin is now jogging. I follow behind. We make our way across the dam. The black water darkens even more with the black clouds above. It's alive with crashing waves and angry whitecaps covering the water's surface. The waves pound the walls, causing water to spray onto our path.

I assume we're running to the other side of the dam, to another vehicle or for shelter, until Adlin stops at the control tower. I follow her onto a steel-gridded platform, old and rusty, probably ready to give way the moment I step onto it. It wraps around the structure and leads to a door. She slams her palm against it three times.

After a few moments, the door creaks open. Paint flakes from the frame and fall through the metal grate below, breaking like icicles dropping from a roof. We step inside, and to my amazement, we're greeted by a tall man in a brown robe. He reminds me of David Carradine in Kill Bill. He walks with a dominating strut, his hands large and powerful. He leans into the door with his shoulder and locks it with a deadbolt, then wedges an old shovel against the handle.

Talk about paranoid.

"Edmond, this is George." Adlin motions to the tall man.

"Nice to meet you, Edmond." I'm surprised by his English accent. He smiles and holds out his hand. I shake it. It's firm and vice-like.

"Hello."

Are there any more people in this weird band? "Is there any more of you?"

"Yes, just one more, Eric," says Adlin, as she pushes and prods the screen of her device.

"That's me," a youthful male voice calls from below, with a Liverpudlian accent. That's weird. I peer over the edge and see the face of a teenage boy looking up at me. He stands among what look like large pumps and other machinery, about forty feet below us. Metal stairs line the wall, spiraling downward.

"Okay, two minutes. Get ready," says Adlin.

George hurries to one of the windows. He looks out and scans the sky. A moment later, Eric arrives from below. He is breathing hard, having just sprinted up four flights of stairs.

"Come on, come on," he says to me as he pulls me toward one of the windows. "You have to see this."

"You must be a fan of the Beatles?"

"The insects?" Eric says frowning. He then smiles, "I love all kinds of insects."

"No, it's a band." I say, staring at him.

He shrugs. "Must be before my time."

I look at Adlin, who is busy fiddling with a box on the wall. Wires hang from it. She takes two of the wires and plugs them into her device. There is a loud static sound that seems to surround us, as if the building had been charged with power. I can hear a subtle hum over the wind outside.

I look out of one of the windows, and there appears to be a blue light glowing from the domed roof above. The light seems to encapsulate the small tower. Beyond it, I see the wild waves. The lightning bursts and flashes outside.

Suddenly, I am shocked to see what looks like a tear in the black sky. It starts to narrow and then grows horizontally, stretching across the sky. Red, pink, and yellow appeared in the tear, like paint were bleeding from behind a black canvas.

"Amazing, different colors every time," says Eric slowly, with a giant smile on his face.

I look at George. The light emitting from above the dome and from the tear in the sky sparkled in his brown eyes and reflect off his shiny complexion.

Then, just like that, the tear evaporates.

"Where did it go?"

"The breach closed. You just peered into another universe," Eric says excitedly. "Cool, eh?"

My brain is overloaded trying to piece this all together. "And what was the blue light on top of the dome?"

Adlin unplugs the device from the wires and slides it into her pocket.

"That was a temporal field I created around us. To protect us from being absorbed into another universe," says Adlin.

"Do you mean if we were out there, we would have been sucked into that thing?"

Adlin purses her lips and looks at me. "Yes."

I turn and look out of the window toward the sky. The black clouds are dissipating, and rays of sun are trying to break through. My throat feels itchy and dry, and my headache has returned. This headache might not be a tumor after all, but heck, my head could still explode with all this madness.

"I need air. I'm suffocating in here. I can't breathe!"

I head for the door.

George beats me there, unbolts it, and yanks it open. I leave the tower and run to the edge of the dam. The air feels cool and refreshing, and I fill my lungs with deep breaths.

Adlin and George join me as we look out over the surface of the water. It's calmer now. The water laps gently against the wall of the dam.

"Guys, you might want to check this out," comes the voice of Eric from behind us. We turn and walk to the other edge.

I can't believe my eyes. As I look down, the landscape is devoid of bushes and trees. Even the fields and pastures are gone. What lies in front of us is another world, one of sand and dust. A desert stretches out for miles and miles before us.

I begin to see stars, everything goes black, and I feel myself falling to the ground. I hear the Beatles song, 'Lucy in the Sky with Diamonds,' playing in my mind. Oooh for the love of George, Ringo, Paul, and John!!

6

Strawberry Fields Forever

I open my eyes to a dark room. A blanket lies on top of me, and the bed feels warm and cozy. For a moment, I wonder if everything has been a dream—Mr. Ringo, the storm, and Adlin.

I then hear faint voices in another room, one female and the other male.

"We have just over fifty-two hours until the parallel confluence," says the female voice.

And it's not a dream, great, it's Adlin and George's voices I hear.

"That means we all need to be in the right place at the right time, with me being first," says George.

I wondered about these mismatched universes colliding with each other. It's such a foreign idea, so absurd, so—stupid. But not impossible; it's just, different.

People who found lodestones earned reverence as powerful wizards. When, in fact, when all it was, was magnetism. Audiences around the world marveled at magicians as they seemed to disappear in a cloud of smoke and then magically reappear somewhere behind the onlookers. People thought they were men of magic and the black arts. It turns out it was something way simpler: the old trapdoor trick. We are so quick to dismiss what we don't understand.

I sit up and swing my legs out of bed. I rub the much-needed sleep from my eyes.

I don't need to understand all the mechanics of this strange situation. I just need to get home. Home to my normal life, my job, and my cat. Is that all I have to go back to?

It's a strange realization I hadn't pondered before. What was the purpose of my life? What friendships had I cultivated? Who would miss me if I were gone? Maybe I should go on a date with Monica?

"Feeling better?" Eric says as he enters the room, snapping me out of my thoughts.

He hands me a bottle of water and what I assumed was a protein bar.

"Keep your strength up. You're gonna need it."

I take a few gulps of water and realize I'm thirstier than I thought.

"What is the parallel confluence?"

Eric furrows his eyebrows and looks at me. "How do you know about that?"

"I heard Adlin talking about it."

Eric smiles. "It's when the perfect circumstances are in place for you, George, and me to return to our respective homes."

I nod my head. "Yes, of course. I figured that," I lied.

Eric slides onto a nearby stool and swung his legs. "It's weird, right? What's your story?"

"My parents are from Merseyside, Kirby to be exact, right off the boat."

"Cool! Home of Lita Roza!" he announces jubilantly. "Nice to know a fellow wool, even if you're not off the boat yourself."

I give way to a little smile. His lingo reminds me of my parents. I miss them dearly.

"And, What do you do in Liverpool?"

"I'm training to be a copper, gonna join the bizzies." He pursed his lips and looks up. "I have a little brother and a little sister who I take care of, along with my grandma. Our parents died in a boating accident."

"Oh, I'm sorry to hear that, Eric." I take a swig of water. "My parents also died when I was young. My mom died of cancer, and my father died in a work accident at the factory he worked."

"What's George's story?"

"Oh, he comes from a weird universe, an alternative dimension. When the USA dropped the Fat Man and the Little Boy on Japan in 1945, there was an atomic chain reaction, creating a different timeline to the history you now know."

"An atomic chain reaction?"

"Yeah. Ninety percent of the world died." He holds up his hand and looks at me through four fingers. "Four continents—unlivable," he says sternly. "Only North and South America and Antarctica are livable now. George said that unless there is a major shift in weather patterns within the next eight years, radiation from Europe and Asia will encroach on the Americas. They're trying to establish small communities in caves and mountains, hoping to survive a little longer. But it means cultivating trees and plant life that would provide the oxygen they need. With no sunlight in the caves, though, it's a challenge."

I take another few gulps of water. I wasn't thirsty. I just needed a few moments to process what I had just heard.

"Sounds like Nevil Shute's novel, On the Beach," I blurted out.

"What?"

"Never mind, just a book I read once."

I try the protein bar. It tastes like a not-so-yummy piece of cardboard.

"I'm sure George is not in a rush to get back home then?"

"Nope, I think he has enjoyed falling into all these different places."

I then had a puzzling thought. "You said, falling into, 'all' these places. How many can there be in one day?"

Eric steps off the stool. "You have only been in this dimension for one day, Edmond. You are at the tail end of our journey. We have been waiting three years for the parallel confluence."

7

Helter Skelter

"We have company!" shouts Adlin in a sing-song kind of voice from the other room.

Eric raises his eyebrows and smiles. "Time to go." He leaves the room. The youngster seems to love all the excitement, the fear, and the action. What do they say, "Foolishness can be mistaken for bravery"?

"Are you coming?" he says, poking his head around the door.

I slip on my sneakers and follow him.

. Adlin and George sport army backpacks loaded down with, I suspect, supplies and other gear synonymous with being on the run: extra clothes, food, tents, and maybe even weapons.

Adlin tosses me some clothes.

"Put these on and grab that backpack," she says, pointing to a bag on the floor.

I welcome the change of clothes. I guessed I was going to need more than just sneakers and pajamas to survive the next step of our outrageous journey. Adlin tosses me a crumpled pair of brown corduroy pants and a mustered-color sweater with the words, Liverpool, across the chest. I assume it's Eric's.

There is suddenly loud banging from the door above. "Who's that?!"

"Government agents," George says.

"The good guys?"

"Not the good guys, Edmond," Adlin says as she attaches a small black box to the wall. She turns to me, one hand still on the box. "They are the kind that will capture, torture, and most likely dissect us."

I don't want to meet those guys. She turns back to the box on the wall and flips a switch. A small green light on the side lights up.

I feel my heart begin to race again. But oddly, not like before. Was I getting used to action? Or was I simply becoming hardened to or desensitized to this new reality?

"What do we do?"

"We run," says Eric as I turn to see him slip an odd-looking gun into a holster on his belt.

"Is that a gun?"

"Just a stun gun," says Eric as he pats the gun handle.

"It's loaded with electrical bullets—tiny slugs, each with a large electrical current. Non-life-threatening," says George.

"Sounds life-threatening."

"Only if I shoot you through the eyeball," Eric says, smiling. He mimicked a gun with his hand and pointed it at me.

"Okay, how do we get out of here?"

Eric yanks open a trapdoor in the floor.

"Eric, twelve minutes," Adlin says, giving him a nod.

Before I can ask what twelve minutes means, we are being ushered into the opening on the floor.

"Let's go, get in."

Eric holds the door open as George disappears down a ladder in the floor. I follow, then Eric. As we descend into the darkness, the light above grows smaller and smaller. The air smells dank and moldy, with a subtle hint of machine oil.

"What about Adlin?"

Although George and Eric seem confident and brave, I figured at some point, like me, they had felt afraid. But their bravery and confidence had been siphoned from another source: Adlin. I find myself trusting her, needing her, and believing she could save us all.

"She will follow. She needs to take care of the agents."

I stop on the ladder. In the dark, Eric's foot touched my head. He pauses, realizing I had stopped.

"Why are you stopping, Edmond?" Eric says.

I protest. "We need to go back. We can't leave her!"

I was surprised at my own words. Was I willing to return to the tower above, no doubt swarming with death agents? For a second, I wondered if I was selfishly worried about my only way back home—or if I was actually worried about someone other than myself. I realized I was beginning to care more about Adlin, George, and Eric than myself. Weird.

"She can take care of herself. We'll only get in the way," George replies from somewhere below me.

His words were wise, no doubt filled with the experience of the last three years.

We push on. Below me, I hear a snap, and then the cavity glows green. George drops a fluorescent green glow stick. It bounces and spins as it hits the rungs of the ladder. Finally, it settles on the floor of the cavity, exposing another thirty feet before we reach the bottom.

We clamber down the ladder and enter a narrow corridor, no bigger than five feet wide. The length of the chamber is difficult to gauge in the dim light of the glow stick.

"This way." George motions for us to follow him. As he holds the glow stick out, I can make out the faint outlines of pipes and metal conduits on the walls.

Finally, we reach a metal door with a large wheel handle.

George grasps the handle and tries to turn it, but it doesn't budge.

Just then, a loud explosion rings out in the distance, causing the walls to shake and vibrate.

Eric looks at his watch and whispers. "That was a quick twelve minutes."

"What just happened?!" I envision this place crushing us to death.

"Adlin has just blown the charges on the internal wall. This chamber will start filling with water."

Okay, so even worse: a slow death by drowning!

"What?! We need to get this door opened, NOW." I was not going to die like this.

"Move George. Eric, let's go. Grab the bottom of the wheel and pull." I pull in the opposite direction.

The water splashed down from the shaft, and it begins to fill the room. It creeps over our feet and ankles. The cold water bites at my toes, causing me to shiver involuntarily. We tug at the wheel. It only moves a tiny amount.

I look at Eric, his young eyes full of wonder and life, too young to die. And George, too wise not to keep sharing his wisdom. The world could use that, and his kindness. I won't let that happen.

"Pull!" I yell.

The water is up to our wastes. Hands slip on the wet wheel.

Finally, it cracks free, and we turn it until the door unlocks. A torrent of water gushes out, sweeping us off our feet. Moonlight bursts through the opening, lighting up the corridor. We gasp as we lie in the water, watching it recede into the ground, and glad to be alive.

In front of us is some kind of barrier, like a frosted bathroom window. It shimmers and moves, almost like water. It stretches as far as we can see, to the left and right.

I look at George and Eric, and then back to the barrier. "What now?"

"Now we walk. Follow me."

Eric takes a few steps forward and holds up his hand. He pushes his arm through the barrier, as if he were reaching through a waterfall. Then he walks straight through and disappears beyond.

"Let's go, son," George says, smiling. He disappears beyond the barrier.

I stand in awe, mesmerized by it.

Suddenly, I heard a zipping noise. I peer into the barrier, but the noise comes from above. I look up to see Adlin sliding down a rope from the top of the dam. Her flowing black jacket makes her look like Batman descending into a street in Gotham City.

She slows as she approaches, then lands just behind me, perfectly—like Black Widow: one knee bent, one leg outstretched, fingertips splayed on the ground. I don't know why I'm thinking of Batman and Black Widow, but that's the vibe she gives off: brave, always in control, as if she knows things the rest of us don't, while we mortals bumble after them like stupid infants who need saving.

She smiles. "You guys got here without drowning, then?"

"Eh yeah. Barely." I let out a nervous laugh.

"And where's George and Eric?" she asks.

I point at the barrier. "Through there."

"So, what are you waiting for? Lets go."

She steps beyond the barrier, disappearing beyond it.

Then I hear the zipping noise again, and by the time I look, it's too late. A man stands ten feet from me, his skin pulled back, his eye sockets dead, dressed in black army fatigues. He has a weapon trained on my head. A rope is still attached to a silver carabiner on his belt.

"Slowly put your hands on your head," he hisses. "Don't make any sudden moves."

I do exactly what he says. I feel my legs shake slightly. What a wimp I am.

He reaches for a radio clipped to his shoulder. Just as he is about to speak, Adlin's fist comes through from beyond the barrier, striking the man in the temple with a loud crack. His knees buckle, and he falls like a tree that has just been cut down.

Moments later, Adlin appears, placing her hands on my back. She pushes me forward into the barrier. My hands and knees are engulfed by sand as I fall forward onto a desert floor.

8

Golden Slumbers

I hate the heat, but this was more than just a hot summer's day. It was like being inside an oven. The heat is intense, and immediately I feel sweat developing on my back and forehead. It didn't seem to bother the others as we trudged across the unstable sand, making each of my steps twice as difficult. I hold my jacket over my head, a crude shield from the blasting ball of fire.

"How far do we need to go?"

Adlin looks at her device and taps a few buttons on the small computer. "Twenty-eight miles."

I immediately stop walking and stare at her. "What?! We can't walk that far. We'll fry in this heat. We need to go back."

Eric chuckled and turns his head while still walking. "And go where?"

I turn. "Back to the..." My sentence trails off, and I'm dumbfounded. Stretching for miles behind us are sand and desert. It lay desolate, only the trail of our footprints shows any reminisce of life or change in the barren landscape.

"Oh yeah, of course," I say sarcastically. "It's changed. We are in another world. How ridiculously stupid of me to think that the very place we just stepped from is still there. I look up to see the others standing looking at me, stupid smiles on their faces. "Yeah, yeah, I know. I'm an idiot." I raise my hands in guilt.

"None of this is normal," George says. "It's just the cards we have been dealt. We can't control the situation we find ourselves in, but we can control how we-."

"React to them," I interrupt. "I know." He sounds like my high school teacher. "Let's go." I flicked a finger forward. "Into the next station of this crazy train we find ourselves on."

Adlin passes a canteen to me. I take a long pull of water. It tastes like the greatest thing I have ever had in my life. I then passed it to George.

"George, what will you do when you return to your world? Eric told me about the radiation's impact on the environment."

George wipes his lips with the back of his hand and passed the canteen to Eric.

"We have tried to build cities deep within the caves."

"Will you be safe from the radiation?"

He gave a half-smile and shrugged. "We don't know. We hope we will be deep enough. We have generators and fresh air supplied machinery. There are heat lamps, which help us grow vegetation, and we have farms and animals."

His words have hope, but his voice is laced with doubt and dread. "You don't seem confident."

"We prepare for the worst and hope for the best. We live every day with our family as if it's our last. I relish those moments, because we don't know how long they will last."

I smile, but I feel sad for him. His warm eyes are kind and wise. It makes me think of my own situation. I have no family, no wife, and no kids. Who would I spend my last moments with at the end of the world? Who would miss me if I were gone? I wonder if I'm the modern-day Eleanor Rigby the Beatles sang about, the lonely person with no friends, dying with no one attending her funeral. I'm suddenly overwhelmed with a feeling of darkness and loneliness, Its tears chunks from my soul.

As the hours pass, I notice I'm acclimating to the heat or the temperature is dropping. But I guess it's the latter. The burning sun is getting low in the sky, and the heat was dispersing from the sand below our feet.

"Getting cooler," says Adlin. "Time to get some miles behind us before dark."

"Shouldnt we get some miles behind us while the sun is down?" A great idea, I thought. I was thinking outside the box. Helping the team. Being an asset, I feel proud of myself.

"Only if you want to freeze your behind off," said Eric.

"Freeze? We are in the desert."

"Yes, we are in the Great Indian Desert, and at night it gets very cold."

Talk about a roller coaster. Hot and cold, like a bipolar Mojave Desert. This was going to wreak havoc on my gentle bones.

In the distance, I think I can see something. I strain to see what it is. It looks like a dark structure growing out of the sand, like a single tooth in a gum line.

I point at the structure. "Look!"

"What is that?" says Eric.

I was glad someone else saw it. It wasn't a mirage, and I wasn't going crazy.

"It looks like." Adlin pauses, squinting in the sunlight. "A castle."

The change of scenery seems to give us all renewed energy. Our pace picks up, and the heat seemed more bearable.

As we draw closer, I can see four large turrets at each corner of the castle. Banners hang from poles attached to the walls at forty-five-degree angles. The banners have red circles on them, but the details are still too far away to make out.

This raises our hopes of shelter, maybe even food and water, but there is still the possibility of unfriendly people, beings, or whatever this place is.

Regardless, we draw closer. This will be our next stop, but it could also be our last.

9

The Continuing Story of Bungalow Bill

The walls of the castle are forty feet high. Arrow slots are strategically placed at evenly spaced intervals halfway up the structure. The four turrets stretch another five feet higher than the walls, giving an optimal view of the surroundings. Not that there was much to see, but miles and miles of golden sand and blue skies.

"What a strange place for a castle," says George, studying the banners, which gently sway in the breeze. They are yellow, with a large orange sun. In the center was a golden cross sitting atop a rock surrounded by water. Vines spread out, hugging the rock and cross. It's a peculiar image.

"It's another bleeding phenomenon," said Adlin nonchalantly.

You don't say. You know, a medieval English castle in South Asia, near a dam, next to my hometown, with the Von Trap family home in its downtown square. Just another day in the life of Edmond Moody.

"I've found a door," exclaimed Eric as he appeared from around the corner. He motioned for us to follow him.

We reach a large, brown mahogany door inlaid with a wrought iron grid-like frame. Chiseled onto the door is the same cross as on the banners.

"Shouldn't we be careful?" Are we assuming the owners of this castle are friendly?"

Adlin turns and raises her eyebrows. "We won't know until we knock."

"Oh, is that how we explore the unknown now? We knock on the doors of strange, scary castles and say, 'Hey, are you my buddy, or are you gonna eat me?' Knock away, let's see if we live to survive the rest of the day." I couldn't help rolling my eyes at the casualness.

Eric smiles and thumps the door with his fist. There's no answer.

I'm suddenly aware of Eric reaching for his weapon. He turns swiftly and fires his gun at what looks like the shadow of a large cat coming towards us. The slug hits the shadow, causing it to shatter into a thousand shards of black glass. Another cat shadow seemed to rise from the sand like a resurrected beast from the grave. The golden sand cascaded off its body. Its green, emerald eyes are the only color on its black surface.

"Get it!" I yelled as I shuffle against the wall.

Adlin fires her weapon, rapidly taking out two of the beasts. But the pact is getting larger, too many of them to fight off.

From above comes a zipping noise; an arrow strikes the cat, shattering the animal. More cats appeared in the sand. To my amazement, the door suddenly opens, and we rush inside.

I didn't know what made me more afraid— the killer cats outside, or the man who stands before us in a black robe and dog collar. He has wavy brown hair and glasses. He stands rigid in his robe with a cross hanging from his neck.

"So, you've met the felines?" the man says with a strong Texas drawl.

"Yes, we did, and thank you for letting us," says Adlin.

There were two loud thuds at the door.

"Can they get in here?" I ask, my voice embarrassingly cracking.

"No. Those evil beasts cannot enter this holy place, for God's hand rests on that door."

We all look at each other, taken aback by his theatrical way of talking.

"I am Father Nemo Pemchan by the way. Welcome."

He's creepy and unnerving.

We stand on a large red rug covering the cobblestones below. On the walls are hand-woven tapestries of an underwater world—plant life, coral, and fish of all colors. They look like paintings made of carpet and are quite remarkable. I've never seen anything so hypnotizing.

The room is lit by various candles, enough to illuminate the room. The enchanting and numinous atmosphere makes the feel of a church.

I notice a noise, subtle, almost like a whisper in the distance. It's a wail, so low I wonder if I imagined it. I look at the others; they seem oblivious. It must have been a breeze, or the noise of the beasts outside.

"These are incredible," whispers George to himself. He studies the tapestries. "May I ask, why the water theme, when you are so far from the ocean?"

"Come, let us ascend," Nemo says commandingly, waving us to follow him up a flight of stone stairs.

We all look at each other, puzzled. We follow the strange priest up the stairs. Eric, of course, leads the way, his curiosity getting the best of him. We spiral around and around and pass rooms where monks are still firing arrows at the cats outside.

Nemo leads us higher, as if ascending to the heavens. We must have been in one of the turrets. Finally, we reach the open air. I look out over the wall to see miles and miles of sand. I turn and can't believe my eyes. In the distance is a faint red scar across the sky. And below was the ocean.

10
Octopus's Garden

A tunnel made of gray and brown rock snaked along from the base of the castle down to the water. It disappears into the ground just before the beach. Forty feet from the shore, the tunnel seems to protrude from the water, like an old water well in a field. Alongside the well is a dock, where a small yellow steamboat with a large paddle wheel on the stern is moored. A red flag blows in the breeze, displaying the same image as the castle flags.

"What's with the tunnel? Why isn't the dock attached to the shoreline?" asks Eric.

"So, the cats don't attack our ship. Felines don't like water," says Nemo.

It made me think of Mr. Ringo. Was he okay back in my world? I realized then that he was the only living thing I cared about back home. A wave of sadness washed over me. If it weren't for my cat, I would be alone. No friends, no family, no wife or girlfriend. Did I push people away? Was that my legacy? Is that how people would view me when I was gone?

Here in this weird world, I met other people. A hero who carried the weight of other worlds and people's survival on her shoulders. A boy who had to postpone his grief for his dead parents to take care of his little brother and sister. And a man whose world was coming to an end, a slow train crash waiting to happen, and nothing in his power could stop it.

And then there is my simple existence, made up of my career and isolation, lined with negativity and self-centeredness, with a cat as my only companion. It was a sad reality. Pathetic, in fact. At that moment, I decided that if I ever get home, I would change that. In fact, I can start now; why wait?

Again, I could hear the wails or cries of something or someone below, coming from the bowels of the castle. Was it the cats, captured and tortured, or something else, something more sinister? There was certainly evil on various levels. But just because one party had a common enemy with another, it did not make them friends. Only allies for a moment to survive another day.

"You didn't come from beyond the sea; you must have come from the sands. Who are you?" asked the Preist.

Adlin answers. "We are travelers."

I assumed the others let her do all the talking when it came to strangers. She always gives the impression that she has a plan and knows everything that was going on.

"You're an odd band of," he paused as if looking for the right word. "Gypsies." He studies up suspiciously now that we are in the daylight.

Just then, three monks appeared from the doorway. They stand silently, as if waiting for a command from Nemo. It gives me an uncomfortable feeling. I look at Adlin, hoping to make eye contact, but she never looks at me. I'm hoping she picked up on the bad vibes I was feeling.

"May I offer you some refreshments and a place to rest? You must be tired from your journey. Here you can be cleansed. It's good for the soul."

"That's very kind of you, but we must be on our way," Adlin says, eyes of determination locked on Nemo.

Nemo raises his hands in protest. His eyebrows bounce behind his glasses. "No, I will not have it. You must allow me to show you some hospitality. Let's eat and talk. Brothers, lead the way."

One of the monks turns and begins to descend the stairs. We follow him, with Nemo and the other monks behind us.

"Something is not right here," I whisper to Adlin.

"I know. Did you notice the tapestries?" She says in a hushed voice.

What is she talking about? I must have missed something. Not very good detective skills, Edmond.

We arrived back in the lobby and head toward another door.

I looked at the tapestries again and finally noticed it. In the corner of the artwork, where the shadows fall, there are images of reeds and seaweed. Among them are the faces of little people. Agony and distress are clear in their eyes. They look trapped, desperately trying to get out of the reeds. The haunting image makes the hair on the back of my neck stand up. Again.

I didn't have to wait long for Adlin to make a move. She throws her foot into the monk in front, sending him barreling down the stairs. She spins and pulls me out of the way, causing me to tumble to the ground. She then fires two shots at the monk behind us. Stunning one and disabling the other.

"Run down and find that tunnel exit!" she yells.

Nemo darts back up the stairs.

Adlin grabs me by the collar and yanks me up. "Go with the others. Find a way out!"

I bolt downstairs as it spirals lower. I can hear the thundering footsteps of George and Eric bolting down the stairs. I suddenly came to a landing and I'm startled to hear a voice coming from an opening in a door.

"Hello, is someone there?" I say, unable to control my trembling voice.

"Help," comes the voice in the dark. It's low and weak, almost a wheeze.

As I approach the door, I see movement behind the barred opening, fingers wrapped around the bars. Above, I can hear gunfire and arrows ricocheting off the stone walls and stairs.

I jump back as a face appears behind the bars, that of a grotesque and deformed man. His deep hollows in his face and disheveled hair make him look emaciated. His teeth have seen better days; black and rotten.

"Help me," the creature pleads.

I look at the handle of the door; a dead bolt lies above it. I place my hand on the cold metal and began to slide it back.

I involuntarily snap my hand back as I hear a forgetful cry from above.

Its Adlin! She sounds distressed.

The mans calmness snaps, and he trashes and screams from behind the door. Froth sprays from his mouth as he snarls through the bars, vicious and evil.

I slowly make my way upward toward Adlin and notice her gun on the stairs. I pick it up, my hand shaking as I feel the cold, hard surface of the grip. But I feel a surge of confidence as it rests in my hand. Staying close to the wall, I creep up the stairs with the gun pointed out in front of me.

Above me stands Nemo with his arm around Adlin's neck. She has an arrow sticking out of her side. She looks pale. Blood runs down her pants leg.

"I'll snap her neck, child, if you come any closer," snarls Nemo.

"Okay, okay." My mouth runs dry, my tongue sticking to the roof of my mouth. "What do you want me to do?"

"Lay down the weapon and allow my brother to take you."

Adlin opens her mouth and lets out a whisper. "Don't do it."

Nemo tugs at Adlin's neck. "Shut up!"

I have to act fast. Adlin is literally dying in front of me, and there's no way I can fire the gun and hit Nemo, or the guard behind him, before he shoots me with that crossbow.

"Okay look. She is dying, and I'm guessing based on that man—or whatever that thing is you have locked up down there—you want a healthy prisoner. Let her go and take me."

Adlin shakes her head slightly. "No."

Am I really about to do this? Did I just offer myself as a sacrifice? I'm shocked at the words that just poured out of my idiotic mouth.

Nemo glances at the monk. It's clear he's considering his options.

"Look, either I run, and you keep an injured prisoner, or we shoot this out and you get nothing. You let her go, and you get me—no fuss, no fight, and a healthy prisoner to do what you wish with. What's it to be, Nemo? I know my friends have found a way out. I can feel the breeze from below."

Nemo purses his cruel lips. "That man down there is unclean, unholy. He needs the Lord's spirit. You all do." He stares down at me like an evil cult leader judging me from the pulpit. "Okay, we trade. This is what we're going to do."

11
Yellow Submarine

"You're going to lay that weapon down and walk my way," Nemo says firmly, motioning toward me.

"No. She's injured, and I need to know she will be safe," I counter.

Nemo rolls his head, cracking his neck. "What do you propose?"

Remembering countless episodes of 24, I have to wing it, Jack Bauer style.

"I am going to come up to you. As I do, you let her go. Only then, will I lay the weapon down on the ground. And you can take me once she is safe in the tunnel."

"Okay," Nemo says slowly, his lips barely moving. A monk stands behind him with his crossbow.

Nemo lets go of Adlin. She stumbles a little and then grabs the railing with one hand while holding her side with her other hand. She grimaces with each step.

"Go, Adlin," I say, encouraging her with a small smile.

I can't believe it is ending like this. I've never sacrificed anything. But here I was, sacrificing not an object, a belief, or a principle, but my very own self.

Adlin eventually moves out of sight. Pemchan moves toward me.

"Hold on, holy boy." I kept the weapon pointed at him and the monk. "A few more minutes. I want her to reach the bottom."

It must have been ninety tense seconds before I laid the weapon down, but it felt like a million hours. Placing the weapon on the stairs is like handing over my freedom. I am overwhelmed with a sense of loneliness and isolation.

As Nemo takes hold of me, I became aware of approaching cries and screams from below. We turn to see the deformed prisoner frantically sprinting up the stairs. His half-human face is flushed red with rage. His eyes are wild and insane.

Whether it was a subconscious reaction to the approaching danger or a flash of opportunity, I instinctively strike out at Nemo with an open hand, thrusting upward into his face, knocking his glasses off. I fire a shot at the guard, catching him in the shoulder. I hesitate momentarily, surprised that I had hit him.

Turning and grabbing the frantic prisoner like a dance partner, I swung him into Nemo and the monk. I sprint down the stairs, sometimes jumping two or three stairs at a time.

"Go go go!!"

I reach the landing to see the prison door wide open. A dank fish smell fills my nostrils. Beyond the landing and down the stairs, I see Adlin struggling to walk. I grab her and begin moving down toward the tunnel, hoping the others will be there to help.

"Nice idea, Adlin, letting the monster loose."

She groans an inaudible reply.

Finally, the stairs end, and we find ourselves in a small rotunda with a low ceiling and a dirt floor. An open door on the far side leads to the tunnel. Lights run along the stone ceiling and disappear around the corner of the burrow.

"Help!" I yell down the tunnel. Adlin is getting heavier, likely because of her rapidly weakening state. I wish I were stronger, another thing I would work on if I ever got out of this mess. To my relief, Eric appears and helps carry Adlin. Together, we hustle down the tunnel. It smells dry and musty, but as the ground steadily rises, I catch the subtle odor of salt air.

The tunnel ends at a set of stairs leading up and over the well onto a dock. A thirty-foot boat lies ahead of us, moored to the dock. The castle sits on the hill behind us.

We scramble aboard the boat.

"Do we even know how to sail this thing? George, you're in the navy, right?"

"Yeah, I think I can sail this contraption," says George. "Detach the tether ropes, Eric."

Eric runs from one end of the boat to the other, releasing each of the ropes attaching the boat to the dock.

George studies the boat's controls, levers, and dials. He notices one of the round dials measures heat, the needle pointed at 100 degrees.

"Come on, George, think," he growled under his breath.

"What is it?" I yell.

"If this thing runs off of steam, which I think it does, we are hours away from getting the heat in the boiler to power that paddle wheel."

I pace. I look at Adlin as she lies on the deck. Eric is studying the wound around the arrow. He needs to remove it and patch her up. Her complexion is pale, and her side is soaked in blood.

This is bad. This is really, really bad.

My mind whirls. Adlin was down, the boat is not moving. We're in a tight spot. We needed to move this boat, even if it was just away from the dock. Think, think, think!

Then it comes to me. If we can't move the boat, then we will move the dock.

"Eric. Do we have any more explosives?"

He looked up, wide-eyed.

"Yes."

"Give them to me! Quick!"

He hands me a black box from his bag and points at a switch on its side.

"This switch will arm the bomb." He then holds up a fob. "This will detonate it once it's armed."

I take the bomb and fob and scramble back down the dock. Excitement soars through me like never before. I feel alive and free. It's euphoric. I place the bomb gently inside the stone well. I can hear the echoes of people running and shouting from inside the tunnel.

Nemo!!

I run back to the boat, and I call for George to throw a rope and tie it off on the boat.

"Get on the dock, Eric. Grab the rope and pull!"

"Edmond, push that button," yells George.

The adrenaline soars through my body, and my ears thud with the beat of my heart like the whooping sound of the blades of an Apache helicopter.

Without looking back, I press the button on the fob. An almighty explosion rocks the dock, causing it to shudder and shake.

"Pull, Eric!"

We both pull on the rope and run. We slowly start gathering speed on the dock, and the small boat begins to budge.

It's working!!

I have never felt so alive as I do right now. I exerted every muscle in my body. It feels painful but exhilarating all at once. Our legs move faster and faster as the boat gathers momentum. The dock begins to sway and becomes unsteady under our feet.

Hold up just a little longer.

"Get ready to jump, Eric."

As we reach the end of the dock, Eric leaps onto the boat. I barely make it aboard myself. My legs burn. We tumble onto the deck of the boat, exhausted and in pain, but we have smiles on our faces.

Behind us, the dock collapses into the water, causing a wave that pushes the boat a little further as it drifts out to sea. The yellow boat stands out against the blue sky and emerald ocean.

George looks down at us both. "We are gonna have a heck of a story to tell Adlin."

12

Red Sails in the Sunset

The dimly lit steamboat sways gently in the water as ripples kiss its yellow hull. Unsure where to go or what to do, George figured out how to release the anchor and dropped it while the boat is two hundred yards from the shore. We will reassess once Adlin is awake.

The stars reflect onto the water, making it look like the boat is sandwiched between two blankets of twinkling stars. It's magnificent, and with no cities or towns nearby, it means zero light pollution. It seems like there were a gazillion more stars in the sky.

We rest and take turns sleeping. We all need the rest. In the morning, I wake up to Eric sitting next to Adlin as she sleeps.

"How is she?"

"She has been talking in her sleep a little, but she seems to be better. The meds have lowered her fever."

That makes me happy. I give Eric a closed-mouth smile.

"Have any of you ever been seriously injured before?"

"I was bitten by a Grogon once. I still have the scar to prove it," says Eric.

I frowned. "A Grogon?"

"It's kind of like a dog, with a titanium exoskeleton, hundreds of tiny teeth, and extremely fast. There was a police organization in one of the worlds we fell into, and they hunted us using the Grogons. Just before the barrier between that world and another opened, I fell over some debris and was bitten in the leg."

"Sounds scary."

Eric shrugged. "Nah, it was fun."

Adlin stirs, and Eric dabs her forehead with a damp cloth.

"Is this all we do is run? What's the plan? I know you say we're waiting for the convergence, but what do we do when it happens?"

These are questions that have puzzled and confused me. Like being lost in a mountain with no map or clear direction.

"Timelines are living things, like tentacles spreading themselves out over time and space."

I frowned and sat down. "Okay. Keep going."

"Eventually, a universe's timeline can become congested, and the membranes of reality begin to deteriorate and collapse. So, in order to protect itself, it branches off and creates another universe timeline that runs alongside it. Eventually, we will have a bunch of timelines and universes piled on top of each other, like the pages of a book. The new timeline will take with it all the history of the past, leaving the present reality with no history. Allowing it to be free of all that data."

Needless to say, I sit and process that for a little while. And needless to say, I fail.

"I don't understand."

Eric adjusts his seating position to face me, as if settling in for the long haul.

"Look, imagine the timeline is like a never-ending bridge full of cars. If bridge A becomes too full, overloaded with cars, or, in this case, data, it will collapse. However, if at some point on bridge A, another bridge, we will call it bridge B, splits off from bridge A, taking with it all the cars from bridge A. In effect, taking the weight off bridge A."

He gestured with pointed hands and waving his arms. It doesn't help.

"But now the two bridges would run alongside one another. Bridge A is now void of history and just the present. And bridge B, with bridge A's history but a new present. The two realities would have similarities, but over time, decisions are made on each bridge/ timeline, creating varying universes."

"Okay, I think I understand." Half of it, at least.

Eric laughs. "I could see the wheels turning behind your eyes."

I start thinking about Back to the Future, Endgame, and Dr. Who, shows and movies that try to explain time travel in layman's terms.

"If history is removed from a timeline, wouldn't the present and the future change since that timeline is based on the past?"

That's a legit question, Edmond. Well done.

"Ah, you would think." He raises a finger. "However, there is something called a permanence of time."

"Believe it or not, I've heard that before! But I don't know what it is."

Adlin stirs again and mumbles something. Eric takes a bottle of water and drips some water onto her chapped lips. The salt air has dried them out, but the water calms her.

"A permanence of time," continues Eric. "Is a fixed time when the universe slits. And the universe picked you as its point of separation."

"Me? Why me?"

"There's no reason. It just happens. For George, it happened in the second half of 1945."

"The bombing of Nagasaki." The words dribble slowly out of my mouth. "When the world changed for George?"

"Yup, he was a permanence of time. The universe split, creating a parallel universe to yours."

"But what about the history?"

"Everything was set in stone at that time. Whatever past actions or events had occurred had been calculated into that universe; therefore, there was no need for all that history and data to sit on the timeline or bridge." He made air quotes with his fingers.

So humans use that silly gesture in other universes. That's annoying. "So, all the history was transferred to George's timeline. With its new posts holding up the bridge?"

"Exactly!"

My head is spinning like a bicycle wheel going downhill, with a rocket attached—on steroids—on ice covered in oil.

This leads to another question.

"Okay, let's say I understand that. Tell me this, how are we all a permanence of time?"

Eric smiles and runs his fingers through his long, black, wavy hair. "You ask all the same questions I asked." He raises a finger. "It's all about checks and balances."

"Say what?"

"When a timeline splits, it creates a permanence of time. When that occurs, a genetic marker is released. In our case, George, his place in the universe is marked. You and I are genetically marked in time and space.

"So, you are saying our destiny was already set?"

"It's not as permanent as it sounds. You and I have still chosen our lives, our destiny, and our own paths."

"But why?"

"Checks and balances. If for some reason there's some crazy collapse of all existence, the universe can reset, based on markers and permanence's of time."

I sit back and think about everything I just heard. The idea was mind-blowing. It made me feel like a tiny speck of pollen whipped in a sandstorm, minuscule and on a quantum level.

George sits down next to us. He looks as tired as we all felt. He holds Adlin's device, rotating it in his hand. "I wish she had shown us how to read this."

"Even if I did, you boys would still be lost without me."

"Adlin!"

She smiles, looking up at us. Color had returned to her face.

"What did I miss?"

13
Sour Milk Sea

I feel the warmth creep into my face as I blush slightly, listening to the guys tell Adlin about my anomalous escapades. I can't quite believe the things they are saying are about me. It sounds like they are talking about someone else—some hero, some amazing human. Not me.

"And then I just got through explaining the whole timeline, permanence of time thingy," Eric says, waving his hands in the air.

Adlin raises her arms. "Help me up."

George and Eric help her to her feet. She winces slightly at the wound in her side. She scans our watery surroundings. The sun reflects brightly off the water, causing her to squint.

"Beautiful. Where are we?"

"No clue. Do we ever know exactly where we are?" I say, smiling.

George chuckled and raises his finger. "This is very true."

Adlin takes her device. "Let's take a look." She presses the screen a few times. "Just under twenty-nine hours."

"I'll start raising the anchor," George says as he pushes off his knees and gets to his feet.

I stand with Adlin, curious about where we were, how her device works, but most importantly, I want to make sure she doesn't fall over the edge, noticing she is still a little unsteady.

She takes some sort of epipen from her bag and rotates the end, making a clicking noise with each twist. "Antibiotics and healing medication," she says, before injecting herself in her side.

Eric passes around those awful protein bars.

What I wouldn't give for a California burrito right now.

"I understand—well, I think I understand—how the timelines and the multiple dimensions work, but I still don't understand what that has to do with me. Where are we going? Why am I, we, so important?"

Adlin fiddles with the device and then studies the shoreline, our location and the elevation of the sun.

"You three have randomly been chosen as markers in time."

"Checks and balances," I say matter-of-factly.

Adlin's eyebrows shoot up. "Yes! George's actions right before the split led to Eric, and Eric's actions directly impact you."

A few days ago, my head was spinning at this, but not now; now my mind is processing the big picture. I had investigated all kinds of things as a PI and at the newspaper. When all the facts, events, paper trails, and players are laid out in front of you, a picture becomes visible. Like a collage of visual information, resulting in an immersive moment of clarity.

"How do you know all this? What is that device?" I ask.

"I'm what's known as a controller. I was actually taken right when I died."

"Died?!"

"Yes. But then given a new life in another timeline."

I stand there, gawking like a fool.

"We are fed information through our dreams, even how to build this device. It has a living organism within it, peeled from the fabric of the universe. It allows me to pinpoint locations where the tears in the universe occur."

"Wow," I say, the only word I'm able to come up with.

"Yeah, it's quite amazing."

"And what happens to you after all this?"

"I will settle down and live my life somewhere. Another controller will take over. Saving all humanity from some other disaster."

I need a drink. A strong one. A double. A triple.

14
The Carnival of Light

The boat sails parallel to the shore. In the distance, we see another tear in the sky. It's low and seems to touch the horizon with its bleeding fingers. Adlin assures us we are at a safe distance from it.

Eric sleeps on a pile of folded-up sails, while George stands at the bow of the boat, keeping the vessel straight. He surveys the clouds and the blue water. I wonder what he's thinking about. Maybe his world, his future, or his family.

"Can't you return George to a better world? I feel like we are simply returning him to a cruel and painful death."

Adlin looks up from her device and looks at me. "He doesn't know yet, but I think I fixed that."

I shift in the chair excitedly. A charge of joy rushes through me.

"Really?"

"That's what I was doing when I saw you at the doctor's office, filling tears and stitching timelines." She wiggles her fingers and grins.

"The guys said you saved the day back there. Thank you."

I waved it off. "It was nothing."

"No, it was something. Your kind of a selfish, negative person, Edmond." She tilts her head and raises her eyebrows. "So, to do what you did back there, willing to give yourself up to Pemchan and put yourself in harm's way—really was quite remarkable."

I fight the urge to take offense at her words, but it quickly diminishes. She's right; I am selfish and can be narcissistic. But Adlin and the others have peeled back a hard mask of egotism and conceit to reveal something soft and kind underneath. Their actions and life experiences have molded me into a man someone could actually love and care about. I began to wonder if Monica had peeked under the corners of that mask, seeing something worth fighting for. Something worth pursuing.

"When I look at others and compare myself, I'm starting to look at how I can improve, and not judge them and or how they can improve as people. It feels good to do the right thing. Is that selfish?"

"Not if others genuinely benefit from it. If you just try for a moment to put others first, people's happiness will bubble up inside of you. Joy and love are two of the most powerful attributes humans possess. No one wants to love a negative person. No one wants to love a hateful person. If you show love, Edmond, love will find you."

"I see something!" yells George. Eric's eyes pop open like a horn went off in his ear.

Eric and I rush to the bow of the boat as George points to some buildings far off in the distance.

Adlin studies her device and then looks up. "George, that's your stop."

I see his head drop, the feeling of impending doom blazing across his face. I place a hand on his shoulder and gently squeeze.

"I think you are going to be okay, George."

George smiles, but behind his eyes, I see gloom.

"George, he's right," Adlin says. "I fixed your timeline. I can't have you die of radiation. It's not in the plan."

"What?" George says incredulously.

"The branch in your timeline has been changed. The chain reaction of nuclear bombs going off will never happen." Adlin comes close to George and kisses him gently on the cheek. "You will continue to live your life, George. You will do great things. I can guarantee that."

15

Being for the Benefit of Mr. Kite

The fringes of a town appear on the shoreline. The buildings becoming less sparse as we move further down the river. The colors of the buildings look like a packet of crayons puked all over the roofs and walls: red, yellow, white, purple, green, and blue. We have to navigate an odd-shaped pier. It's uneven, with one end higher than the other. Even the wooden beams that enter the water vary in thickness.

"What kind of drunk builders constructed this thing?" George says as he maneuvers our yellow boat alongside the dock.

"Probably Irish," I mumble.

Once the noise of the steam engine dies down, we hear music faintly playing in the distance, if you can call it that. It sounds like random noises all thrown together in some twisted song.

Eric tests the stability of the pier before we disembark from the boat. It holds firm, clearly built to last. We make our way up a ramp and are amazed to see the town before us. Avant-garde-style buildings line the burgundy cobbled streets. Some structures lean more toward brutalism than avant-garde, with straight lines, hard, sharp angles, and no curves at all. One building looks like it's made entirely of Lego blocks—windowless and perfectly square. Others resemble the pier itself: off-kilter and uneven. Still more look like combinations of two or three toy buildings fused together, as if mashed by a giant, deranged toddler.

Couples walk hand in hand; others walk alone, or with pets, or canvas shopping bags. Their dress is equally avant-garde, giant, colorful jackets and exaggerated shoes. Some wear tall hats in various colors, paired with flat, shapeless shirts or jackets, as if made of cardboard rather than cotton or wool.

People glance at us and laugh, monition toward our strange clothes. We must look silly and foreign to them. Strange music still drifts in the distance, perhaps from a fair or circus somewhere far off.

"What a fun place," says Eric. His smile is contagious, and I smile too.

We saunter around and marvel at the deeply abnormal surroundings. It was as if modern art was feeding off magic mushrooms and spawning this odd town, like a mole on the back of traditionalism.

Each building, outlandishly challenging the normal aesthetics of what was normal.

A group of people in yellow pajamas and white bonnets danced and laughed as they approached us. A young lady with giant eyelashes and green hair stopped, made a mockingly sad face at me, and then pushed a paper flyer into my chest.

"Go, you strange fellow, you will have fun." She then laughed hysterically, spinning away into a dance.

I study the flyer and its images of a circus tent with clowns and a strong man with a handlebar mustache flexing his muscles. A troop of monkeys sit on the back of an elephant, led by a clown that looked remarkably like Bozo. The words, in various fonts and sizes, describing the event, cascaded down the page, swirling around the images.

Eric snatches it from me and studies it, his face full of wonder and excitement.

"Let's go!" he exclaims.

Adlin sighs and rolls her eyes. Babysitting us must be exhausting.

"Let's just get George to where he needs to be. I'm sure he is eager to see his family and new world," I say to Eric.

"Well, how long do we have?" George says. Adding a couple more centimeters to Eric's already overly extended smile.

Adlin looks at her device and raises her eyebrows. "We have about three and a half hours before the next bleed. We can kill some time, I guess, in this topsy-turvy world."

Eric looked around for someone and then ran to a man dressed in an oversized white pinstriped suit. He is a little startled at first until Eric shows him the flyer. He then points, clearly giving directions.

Eric summons us to follow him. We make our way down what seems to be the main street of the town. We arrived at a row of large animal statues made entirely of various colored flowers. Behind them is a field with a giant circus tent in the center, surrounded by artists and exhibitionists performing tricks and balancing acts. People huddled around them, fascinated.

Apart from the weird avant-garde people and out-of-the-ordinary landscape, it was a normal looking, traditional fair.

Something had been bothering me ever since we were aboard the boat. Adlin had said it wasn't in the plan to have George die. I figured there were some things Adlin was not revealing to us. Maybe for our own safety, too much knowledge had the ability to change or affect timelines and universes. Dr. Who taught me that.

George and Eric were now walking together, looking at the jugglers and performers, pointing and laughing. Adlin and I strolled behind them.

"You had said that it wasn't in the plan for George to die. Do you have a plan?"

"Kind of."

"Kind of?" I turn to look at her. "That's vague."

"It's complicated, Edmond."

We separated as we walked around a group of people sitting on the ground, watching a puppet show. It was a weird, trippy Mr. Punch and Judy show.

I rejoined Adlin, and we resumed our conversation.

"Then, un-complicate it." I'm not giving up.

She studies me with her wise eyes, reading my mind and face, peering into my soul and heart, knowing I won't stop asking.

"You know, Edmond, there are things in your world that are unmovable, permanent things or events that mold human expansion and society. Like the Ice Age, the Spanish flu, and the invention of penicillin. How often do you think of the Roman Empire?"

All the time.

"Every week, right?"

Three times a week.

"Even people," Adlin continues. "Einstein, Napoleon, the Wright brothers. Like the coupling of a train, without the links, the individual trains would no longer be connected."

"Okay."

"There are actions that are like links leading to major events or people."

"And we are those?"

"Basically, yes. Eric plays a part. George plays a part. You and I play a part."

"And it molds history."

She nods. "Yes."

"What do they do? What do I do?"

"It affects the type of love in the world."

"Love? So not stopping a serial killer from killing dozens of people, or World War Three?"

"Love is more powerful, Edmond."

We are both distracted as we walk by a dwarf with a sword down his throat, juggling five flaming knives. It's actually quite impressive, and it steals my attention. After a few more minutes,

George and Eric say they are ready to go and we head back to the center of town.

Adlin leads us down a narrow lane. The walls are lined with triangular and hexagonal windows.

At the end of the lane sits a small water fountain. It's fairly unremarkable, except for its bright colors. The yellow pool is small, with a striped red-and-white beam protruding from the center. Water cascades from a hidden hole at the top of the square-shaped column. We rest on the pool wall and look at the houses surrounding the fountain. One in particular looks odd; it's shaped like a crooked cylinder with a cone on top, made entirely of copper.

"This is it, George. You're going home," Adlin says.

"And it's a new world?" He struggles to speak, hesitating, in case he breaks the spell of a promised new life.

"Yes, George," Adlin says as she places her hand in his.

"How long?" I ask glancing down at Adlin's device.

"Fifteen minutes."

"Ta'ra for now, George," Eric says as he holds out his hand. "It's been a wild ride, my friend.

I'm glad you are not going back to that rotten world of cave dwelling and radiation."

George shakes Eric's hand and graciously bows his head slightly. "Me too. Take care, son."

Adlin smiles at George and then gives him a huge hug. They hold each other, locked in an embrace of friendship, and neither one willing to let go.

"It's time," Adlin says after a few moments.

"How does this work?" Eric asks.

"George, you will stay right here. But we need to leave. We will be just over there." She points to the copper house. "I will use that as a temporal field."

I shake George's hand. I get a tingle of warmth and kindness from his handshake. It's been two days, but he feels like a brother, bonded together by shared trails and tribulations. I'm not quite sure why I am drawn to him the way I am. Like Adlin, there seems to be some sort of magnetic pull to them both. I don't feel it with Eric, even with his amazing Liverpudlian accent.

The sky starts to rip open; blues and grays flash through, forming the gaping tear.

Adlin rushed us to the copper house and energized the temporal field around the house with us nearby.

George coughs, his face turning red. He sweats and pulls at his collar.

"Is he okay?" I say, panicking.

"Yeah, it's normal. Remember, it happened to you," Adlin says.

Ah yes, the whole absorption into another universe deal.

And just like that, George is gone, lifting an enormous weight off my shoulders. Not only is George safe in his new world, but it makes me feel closer to mine.

Adlin lets out a deep breath. The sheer exhaustion must be overwhelming. "Eric, we need to be ready for you. But for now, I think we can all use some rest."

We find an empty house, and Adlin jimmies the door. She has many skills. And I guess breaking and entering is one of them.

We each take a bed. I didn't realize I was so tired until my head hit the pillow.

16
Revolution 9

Three men stand behind a glass window, like a lineup at the police station. It's Eric, George, and Nemo. Nemo has the Bible hanging from his neck. But the front is blurred out. They each hold a small black sign up in front of them with their name printed in white.

I look from behind the class. Although I know them all, they seem like strangers, actors playing roles in a play.

I then suddenly find myself standing on a sidewalk. Identical brown houses line the road. Kids play hopscotch and soccer around me like I'm invisible. A ghost. The old parked cars look British, I'm guessing around the 1950s or 60s.

I blink and I'm now standing on a street corner in what looks like New York City. Across the street is a large sandstone building. Balconies with balusters and archways grace the structure. A great archway, twenty feet high, leads into the building's interior courtyard. A black wrought-iron gate blocks the entryway.

I realize it's the famous Dakota apartments, and I'm staring right at the very spot where John Lennon died.

I'm back at the line-up again, looking at Eric, George, and Nemo.

Nemo Pemchann, why does that name seem familiar? And why Nemo? Nemo is the guy from Jules Verne's Twenty Thousand Leagues Under the Sea. And Pemchan—what kind of name is that?

Pemchan, Chenpam, Champen. Then it hits like a ton of bricks, John Lennon's killer. CHAPMEN!! Mark David Chapmen!! He was also called Nemo by kids at a YMCA he worked at. I look at the men again. The book cover hanging from Nemo's neck is no longer blurred. And it's not a Bible. It's a copy of The Catcher in the Rye.

The whole cleansing thing, and godlike complex back in the castle- Mark Chapman. It all made sense now. But who were Eric and George. Why the British neighborhood?

17
Blue Jay Way

My eyes shoot open like a startled cat in the unlit room. A shaft of moonlight casts itself onto the patchwork rug on the floor. Good to know there is a moon in this wacky world too. I hear Eric gently breathing in the next room. I can't stop thinking about the dream. I go over and over in my head Adlin's words about how George fits into a "plan." And "the type of love in the world," and, "events that mold human expansion and society." Sure, John Lennon's death was monumental and affected a lot of people, but all this nonsense can't have anything to do with John Lennon. My brain must has weaved a dream from all these crazy multiverse threads.

I rack my brain as to George and Eric. George is not George Harrison; I know that. Then I remember the fifth Beatle, George Martin! He pushed and molded the Beatles to be the best they could be, mixing their songs and even playing on many of their albums. Adlin reinserting him into a new world, maybe his original world before the bombing, would ensure the Beatles' success, and thus molding the world with their songs of love.

I dart out of bed, whipping the covers off, and rush to where Eric is fast asleep. I shake his shoulders.

"What is it! What is it!" he yells, confused eyes staring up at me.

"You've never heard of the Beatles? How can that be? You're from Liverpool!"

He pulls away from me as he gets up. "What are these Beatles you keep asking me about? No, I've never heard of them."

I stare at him. "When were you born?"

"1934. Why?"

I stroll around the room trying to piece all this together like some mad lawyer in a courtroom. Most of the Beatles are younger than him, then. Could he be a musician, a sound engineer, a producer like George, someone impactful to the Beatles and their music? I'm vaguely aware that the light in the room from the moon has changed to a light green hue. I ignore it as my investigator mind races.

"Are you a musician? Do you play any musical instruments, Eric?"

He looks at me like I've lost my mind. Maybe I have, days ago.

"I tinkered around with a banjo one summer. But my father was in the bizzes, and I guess I was following in his footsteps of being a copper."

"We have a problem!" says Adlin as she bolts into the room.

"What?" I snap.

"Look outside."

We rush to the window. A large green smog fills the air, barely allowing the moonlight through. The moon looks like a dirty green lightbulb.

"Eric has twenty-two minutes to get to his location!"

I turn to Adlin. "I thought we had at least ten hours!"

"Something has shifted."

"What do you mean, how?"

"Has anything happened out of the norm?" she asks, her tone serious.

"None of this is the norm!" I say irritably.

Adlin raises her hand at me. "Okay, okay. We need to go. NOW!"

We gather our supplies.

"Leave it. Leave everything!" she snaps.

This is bad. I've never seen her like this. She is flustered and panicked. A sense of worry wells up in my bones. The once strong stone tower, Adlin, where we sought protection, is now a weak, flimsy garden shed.

We rush from the house and chase Adlin as she darts down alleyways and over roads. The air reminds me of those old movies set in London when everything was foggy from all the coal fires. Except it's green, like the smoke from some Celtic genie's lamp. That will be next!

"Fourteen minutes," she shouts breathlessly.

My shins and thighs start to burn and ache. Eric is sprinting between Adlin and me, seemingly with endless energy. So, he's not a musician. He's learning to be a copper.

We reach a metal bridge lit up by rows of glass animal statues. Inside them are lights, illuminating the bridge.

A bright white light glows through the green fog. I sense the sky opening.

Adlin suddenly stops at the start of the bridge. She's breathing hard. She looks at her device.

"Eric, right here!" She pointes at a spot on the ground. "Seven minutes."

I look at the young boy's face and can't believe this is it. It feels rushed, meaningless, and unfair to say goodbye so quickly.

I hug him tightly. A piece of him reminds me of George. I break away, and Adlin hugs him too.

"Goodbye, Eric," she says.

"Thank you both for what you have done. And thank you, Adlin for fixing all this." He cries, making me well up too.

The fog is turning whiter as the light gets brighter, penetrating the green fog.

"We need to get onto the bridge, Edmond."

We rush onto the bridge and turn to look at Eric. Adlin uses two wires and her device to energize the bridge. A blue glow surrounds us. Then I'm struck by an overwhelming moment of clarity. Eric, is Eric Clague.

"It's him," I say quietly in disbelief. "It's him."

"What?" says Adlin.

"I need to stop him from going back to his world."

Adlin turns and faces me, putting herself between me and Eric. "Edmond, what are you saying?"

"I said, I need to stop him. He is the guy who killed John Lennon's mom. He hit her with his car. Speeding." The words burn in my mouth.

"Edmond, listen to me." She holds out her hand, almost touching my chest. "It needs to be this way."

"It doesn't!" I can't help but growl the words.

"If John's mom isn't killed by Eric's car in 1958, then John Lennon never writes "Mother," and "Julia," and a whole butch of other songs. He would cease to be the John Lennon we know, and that means no Beatles."

She is now pushing against my shoulders; I resist, and look over her shoulder at Eric. I don't even know what I would do if I got ahold of him. Hit him? Kill him?

Adlin pleads with me, anguish on her sweaty face. "All the pain and hurt that seventeen-year-old John goes through makes him the great artist he was. It's a bittersweet truth. His songs of love and joy were born in the burning ashes of hurt and pain. The Beatles' songs spread love, Edmond. A joy and love the world has never seen. It needs to be this way."

Rationality slowly seeps back into my cells and brainwaves. I begin to let Adlin push me back, no longer fighting, no longer resisting.

Eric stands with his back to us, looking up at the sky and begins coughing. He rubs his temples.

The signs of universe bleed. The light has completely transformed the green fog into white fog. He turns and waves at us. And then, just like that, he vanishes.

18
Two of Us

The fog lifts fast, exposing the river below the bridge. The statue lights are gone now, and it's just regular old bridge lights as they reflect off the gently flowing water below.

"Did you figure out who Nemo was?"

I stare into the water at the leafs as they float by. "I had a dream about Chapmen and Nemo and John's Lennons Dakota apartment in New York. Then, when I woke, I figured out who George was. Then, finally, Eric."

"That's why the Permanence of Time came so close to George's. It shifted." She wags her finger up and down. "Too much knowledge of the past and present. It messes with the laws. That's why I couldn't say anything."

"So, when's my time?"

She unhooks the device from the bridge and pushes and prods the screen. "Thirty-eight minutes."

"Where? Let me guess, we need to run there?"

"Nope." She smiles. "The other end of the bridge."

Shocker!

"Shall we?" she says, mentioning along the bridge.

We walk slowly, and for a few minutes neither one of us says a word. I'm not sure if it's shock or exhaustion.

"I just can't believe that all this has to do with the Beatles." I shake my head, trying to move all the pieces around in my head, hoping to finish the jigsaw. It's hopeless.

"It's just the way it is, Edmond. The universe has a weird way of processing things and figuring out problems. We can't control the universe. But we can-."

"Control how we react to it." I say, finishing the sentence. "I know, I know."

"You know, Edmond, I think when you get back home. You should call that girl. What's her name, Monica?"

I stop and look at her, my eyes wide open. "Okay, I don't care what you say, but you were— stalking me!"

We both laugh and continue walking.

"Yes, I think that's a good idea." I admit.

We reach the end of the bridge and sit on the ground. It's then that I notice the road has giant white lines painted on it. Exactly like a zebra crossing on Abbey Road. I smile and enjoy the moment.

"Did you know the Abbey Road album is the only Beatles album to have no writing on it? And that a policeman held up the traffic for ten minutes while a photographer took the picture on top of a stepladder?"

Adlin smiles and nods. "Did you notice Paul wears no shoes in the picture?"

My smile widens. "Yes, I did!"

"They don't fit him," she says.

The fog has lifted now, and the sun is only showing it curve on the horizon. I look out at our surroundings and realize we are in London, or at least an odd version of it. I see Big Ben and the Shard in the distance. St. Paul's Cathedral is off to the left, and London Bridge is behind it.

"Three minutes, Edmond."

"Oh, no crazy lights or tears in the heavens?"

"Nope, this is the end, and we are close to your universe."

We stand. Adlin kisses me before throwing her arms around me. I don't want to let go. I start to cry. How embarrassing! I wipe my sniffling nose.

She steps off the bridge and energizes a small metal bench at the side of the road and sits on it. I cough and can feel an oncoming headache.

"Hey, how did you know Paul's shoes don't fit him?" I call out between coughs to Adlin.

"Because I was there, and he told me."

My eyes feel like they will pop out of my head. I stand there speechless. I can feel my body being absorbed or pulled or whatever. I don't know.

Adlin is an anagram of Linda. Linda McCartney.

I find myself in my office at work. Music plays somewhere out in the lobby. It's the work party from a few days ago. Right before I got sick. Well, not sick. But you know what I mean.

There's a knock at the door. I open it to see Monica standing there with two red solo cups.

"Time to stop working, Edmond, and come and enjoy the party."

I've never noticed it before, but she is actually quite beautiful. I can't help but smile at her. She smiles back at me. Just then, a Beatles song started to play in the background.

"Wanna dance?" I say.

"Sure, it's my favorite song."
"Me too."

The End

About the author

Robbie was born in Oban, Scotland, but now lives in the USA.

He has published six books. His short stories have been published in various online and paperback formats internationally.

He is married and works full time as a quality manager in the Boston area.

Please consider writing a review on Amazon or Goodreads, and, please share with EVERYONE YOU KNOW!

Please visit my website www.robbiesheerinwriter.com to learn more about me and my previous work and sign up to my mailing list or send me a message.